BOOK

Written by Florence Meurée
Translated by Carly Probert

The Diary of Anne Frank

BY ANNE FRANK

Bright
≡Summaries.com

ANNE FRANK

GERMAN AUTOBIOGRAPHER

- **Born in 1929 in Frankfurt, Germany**
- **Died in 1945 at Bergen-Belsen**
- **Her work:**
  - *The Diary of Anne Frank* (1947), autobiographical novel

Of German origin, Anne Frank (1929-1945) is a symbol of the persecution and extermination of Jews that took place under the Nazi regime. The rise of anti-Semitism and the multiplication of Anti-Jewish laws in the 1930s forced her family to emigrate to the Netherlands before going into hiding.

The family business, located in the center of Amsterdam, served as a hiding place for two years for a total of eight Jews. Anne, whose ambition was to become a writer or a journalist, wrote her diary there as well as stories and works of fiction, which were published in 1982 and revised in 2003, under the title *Tales from the Secret Annex: Stories, Essay, Fables and Reminiscences Written in Hiding*.

Likely to be the result of a betrayal, the family was arrested in August 1944 and deported to the Bergen-Belsen concentration camp. Anne fell ill with typhus and died in the winter of 1944-1945.

THE DIARY OF ANNE FRANK

THE DIARY OF A CONDEMNED YOUNG GIRL

- **Genre:** Personal diary
- **Reference edition:** Frank, A. 2001. *The Diary of a Young Girl: The Definitive Edition*. Reprint edition. Bantam.
- **1st edition:** 1947
- **Themes:** World War II, anti-Semitism, secrecy, friendship, deportation, fear

In 1947, Otto Frank took the initiative of publishing his daughter's diary under the title *The Annex*. The distinctive feature of this text is that it was originally intended for strictly personal use: Anne tells of her daily life in hiding with all the constraints that it involved. She also indulges in reflections on her personality, her relationships with others, and the war.

The Diary of Anne Frank is one of the most read books in the world with twenty-five million copies sold and translations into fifty-five different languages.

SUMMARY

BEFORE GOING INTO HIDING

The diary begins on 12th June 1942, the day of Anne's 13th birthday. The diary is one of the birthday gifts she receives. The young girl then leads a quiet life in Amsterdam: she spends her time with her school friends, gets punished in class for being too talkative and has several admirers that do not interest her.

Along with these teenage concerns, there are those linked to the context of the time. Anne mentions the anti-Jewish laws implemented by Hitler that are being applied to the occupied Netherlands (wearing the star is mandatory, Jews are banned from using public transport , from visiting entertainment venues and from visiting the houses of Christians, etc.).

GOING INTO HIDING

In early July 1942, Otto, Anne's father, tells her that they will soon be going into hiding. Their departure, originally scheduled for 16th July, is brought forward by one week due to an alarming event: Margot, Anne's older sister, receives a call-up to work in a camp in Germany: "I was stunned. A call-up: everyone knows what that means. Visions of concentration camps and lonely cells raced through my head [...]" (Wednesday 8th July, 1942).

The next day, the Frank family moves to the 'Annex', which is the unused parts of Otto's business, without knowing that they will remain there for over two years. The employees of Anne's father (Miep, Bep, Kleiman and Kulger) know about the secret. They will take care of supplying provisions for those in hiding. Anne feels that her carefree life is well and truly over. But it is still difficult to consider the hiding place as her new home.

The Van Daan family, composed of one of Otto's associates, his wife and their son, joins them on 13th July. The Franks learn that there are various rumors circulating about their sudden disappearance. At first, Anne is thrilled with the arrival of these new occupants, but tensions arise very quickly: "I think it's odd that grown-ups quarrel so easily and so often and about such petty matters" (Monday 28th September, 1942).

Anne often finds herself at the center of these arguments, with the Van Daans accusing her of being too talkative and pretentious. The girl also has conflictual relationships with her mother and sister, to whom she feels very different.

AN EIGHTH PERSON

In November, the Annex welcomes a new occupant: Albert Dussel, a dentist. He settles in Anne's room.

From the window, she regularly witnesses the roundups of Jews. She feels guilty for being able to sleep in a bed every night while so many people are being arrested and deported: "[...] I can't help thinking about those who are gone. I catch myself laughing and remember that it's a disgrace to be so cheerful" (Friday 20th November, 1942).

All those in hiding turn their thoughts to the fate of the Jews and the progress of the war, but they are also concerned with certain events that affect them directly. They fear that the new owner of the building will want to visit the Annex; they do not trust the new shopkeeper who could expose them; they are terrified at the idea of being discovered during a burglary; they fear for their life during every bombing or air combat.

Some personal troubles also punctuate their existence, such as the lack of money which forces the Van Daans to resell some of their clothing and Anne's short-sightedness.

Aside from that, the days follow in a certain monotony, to the point where Anne dedicates some diary entries to describing the evenings, nights and meals in the Annex. The only distractions they have are the radio, reading books and newspapers, and studying (shorthand, French, English, etc.). Anne loves history, mythology, royal genealogy and cinema most of all. She also devotes part of her time to writing fiction.

A SPECIAL RELATIONSHIP IN THE ANNEX

Anne feels misunderstood and often cries in bed at night. The need to ease her pain leads her to confide in Peter. She visits the young man's room more and more regularly, despite her fear of disturbing him.

The two teenagers talk about various topics, ranging from their personality to sexuality, all the way to their relationship with their parents. They also look out of the window in silence. Initially, Anne claims not to be in love with Peter as she loves another boy of the same name, whose apparition in a dream affected her deeply: "It seems as if I've grown up since the night I had that dream, as if I've become more independent" (Saturday 22nd January, 1944). However, the friendship the young girl feels for her fellow hider quickly evolves into stronger feelings: "In the meantime, things are getting more and more wonderful here. I think, Kitty, that true love may be developing in the Annex" (Wednesday 22nd March, 1944). This leads to her first kiss.

On Tuesday 28th March 1944, Minister Bolkesteyn announces on the radio that evidence in the form of letters and newspapers will be collected after the war. As a result, Anne begins rewriting her diary: "Just imagine how interesting it would be if I were to publish a novel about the Secret Annex. The title alone would make people think it was a detective story" (Wednesday 29th March 1944).

In April, they are almost discovered following another burglary: the night watchman, having noticed a hole in the door, inspects the interior of the building with the help of a policeman.

A TRAGIC END

Anne experiences a period of despondency: "I feel more miserable than I have in months. Even after the break-in I didn't feel so utterly broken, inside and out." (Friday 26th May 1944). She then regains her courage when she learns that the landing had begun: she follows the progress of the English daily.

The last letter in the diary is dated 1st August 1944. It talks about Anne's hidden personality, which she never reveals, and which, according to her, is more beautiful and deeper than the one she shows to others. Three days later, they are arrested.

CHARACTER STUDY

ANNE

Born on 12th June 1929, Anne is the youngest of those in hiding. On reading her letters, we soon realize that she is talkative and loves to be noticed (Sunday 21st June 1942). These traits of her character provoke strong reactions from the adults. Anne does not show it, but in reality she is deeply saddened by all of these reprimands ("I wish I could ask God to give me another personality, one that doesn't antagonize everyone", Saturday 30th January 1943).

Due to the particular living conditions, the girl quickly acquires a high level of maturity: between the first letters exposing stories about her classmates and the last, where she covers topics such as sexuality, human nature or the condition of women, the contrast is striking.

Anne's ambition was to become a writer or journalist. She wanted to live on after her death (Wednesday 5th April 1944). Her wish was to come true since her name would be known throughout the entire world.

EDITH FRANK

The relationship between the mother and daughter is particularly tense. There is no complicity between them and they regularly argue. For Anne, Edith represents the opposite of what a mother should be. The teenager feels as though she has to educate herself ("[...] I miss - every day and every hour of the day - having a mother who understands me", Friday 24th December 1943).

On several occasions, Anne speaks harshly of Edith (Saturday 3rd October 1942, Friday 17th March 1944), but in the letter dated 2nd January 1944, she recognizes her own wrongdoings and relativizes ("The period of tearfully passing judgment on Mother is over. I've grown wiser and Mother's nerves are a bit steadier."). Edith is not immune to this problematic relationship with her daughter, as illustrated by her tears when Anne refuses to pray with her (Friday 2nd April 1943).

OTTO FRANK

Anne's father was the director of the company Opekta, where they go into hiding. Anne holds him in high esteem, and sometimes thinks he is the only member of the family who understands her. He is very optimistic, calm and never complains.

Anne seeks refuge from him whenever there is a bombing. In everyday life, he helps his daughter to study her lessons and it is him that the others turn to when a decision needs to be made.

It also happens that Anne feels misunderstood and abandoned by her father, as is evidenced in the letter she writes to him ("When I was having problems, everyone - and that includes you - closed their eyes and ears and didn't help me.", Friday 5th May 1944.

Otto was the only one of the eight people in hiding to survive the deportation. After the war, he remarried and moved to Switzerland, where he lived until his death in 1980.

MARGOT FRANK

Three years older than Anne, Margot has a very different personality from that of her sister: she is discreet, almost faded, and never finds herself the subject of disputes. She also proves to be very gifted in her studies. Irony and jealousy are apparent when Anne calls her a 'model girl'.

At times, Anne cannot stand her sister and feels as though her parents do not treat them both the same way ("Is it just a coincidence that Father and Mother never scold Margot and always blame me for everything?", Saturday 7th November 1942). On the other hand, a certain complicity develops between the two girls at times (Anne allows her to read a few passages from her diary).

After the war, Margot wanted to become a pediatric nurse in Palestine. She also kept a diary which was never found.

PETER VAN DAAN (VAN PELS)

Prior to 1944, Anne had no affinity with Peter. She finds him oversensitive, lazy and uninteresting ("a shy, awkward boy whose company won't amount to much", Friday 14th August 1942). His extreme shyness means he is very quiet.

Later, Anne finds in him a confidant. She spends almost every afternoon in his company and ends up falling in love with him. Peter admits that he lacks self-confidence. He admires her for her confidence and her quick comebacks. In her final diary letters, Anne explains how she is disappointed in Peter because of his aversion to religion and his weakness of character.

Peter planned to visit the plantations of the Dutch East Indies.

MR. AND MRS. VAN DAAN (VAN PELS)

The husband and wife are often noted for their arguments. Their behavior sometimes annoys Anne, for example when they save the best parts for themselves at the table.

Mrs. Van Daan handles the kitchen. She is cheerful, but Anne finds her unbearable when she complains about her or makes a remark about her upbringing. As for Mr. Van Daan, he likes to offer his opinion on everything and becomes very irritable when he runs out of cigarettes.

ALBERT DUSSEL (FRITZ PFEFFER)

He is the last to enter into hiding in the Annex and is the only person unaccompanied by his family. His partner, a Christian, does not need to live in hiding. Anne has to share a room with him, which she is not pleased about. Like Mrs. Van Daan, the dentist believes that Anne is ill-mannered.

Anne is irritated when she discovers that he has a personal supply of food and she believes that he sometimes lacks caution (he asks Miep to bring him a pamphlet on Mussolini and does not support the new security measures taken following the burglary). The other people in the Annex make fun of his memory loss and the promises that he never keeps (Wednesday 17th November 1943).

THE PROTECTORS

Four people watch over those in hiding: Kleiman and Kugler, put in charge of the Opekta company, Miep, the secretary and Bep, the office worker. The daily assistance they provide is precious to the inhabitants of the Annex. They bring food, books and try to provide for their material needs. They bring them news from the outside world and cheer them up with their daily visits. Those in hiding are aware that they are completely dependent on them. Anne is extremely grateful to these 'heroes' who risk their lives to help them (Friday 28th January 1944).

ANALYSIS

HISTORICAL CONTEXT

In 1919, after World War I, the Treaty of Versailles was signed. It aimed to establish peace between the victors of the war and Germany. The latter was forced to relinquish its colonies and some of its territories.

Ten years later, the world was shaken by the stock market crash that occurred in the United States and led to the period known as the Great Depression. It plunged the world into a deep crisis, during which the rates of poverty and unemployment rose sharply. As a consequence, this led to the rise of totalitarian political parties (parties that hold all the power and accept no opposition), such as Nazism in Germany, fascism in Italy and Francoism in Spain).

In Germany, Hitler was at the head of the German Workers' Party in 1920, which he renamed the National Socialist German Workers' Party. Thanks to the personality of its leader and the economic and social contexts, it became the first party from 1932 onwards. A year later, Hitler took power of the country. He then launched a series of exclusionary measures against the Jews, taking a census of them, forcing them to wear the yellow star, dismissing them, deporting them and even having them murdered. He considered the 'German race' to be superior to others and thus wanted to eliminate the Jews, the Roma, etc., that threatened his intentions for an 'Aryan race'. It was for this reason that the Frank family decided to leave Germany in 1933 and travel to the Netherlands, which had declared itself neutral when the conflict broke out and which had, thus far, been spared.

Unfortunately, in May 1940, the country was invaded by Germany who enforced a political regime for repressing the Jews. They were threatened with being sent to concentration camps if they were deemed fit for work, where they were treated inhumanely, or to extermination camps where they were killed in the gas chambers. Some people chose to oppose the German invasion and help the Jewish community (hiding them, giving them food, etc.). These were called the 'resistants' and risked a death sentence if discovered.

It was not until May 1945 that the Netherlands was liberated from the German yoke, after numerous battles that resulted in the deaths of tens of thousands of people.

LIFE IN HIDING

The Diary of Anne Frank can be considered a historical document on the living conditions of life in hiding during the Second World War. Indeed, the Franks needed to completely reevaluate their lifestyles once they moved into the Annex. Although Anne believed they were very fortunate compared to the deported Jews and that they were more comfortably settled than the majority of people in hiding, her letters do show how painful life in hiding must have been, for several reasons:

- The complete dependence on others. Their lives were no longer fully in their hands, they had to rely on their protectors. When one of them fell ill, this had consequences on their existence. Moreover, they depended on the fate of the providers of their ration cards and on Van Hoeven, who provided them with potatoes. When he was arrested, Anne wrote that there was nothing they could do except eat less (Thursday 25th May 1944);

- Material constraints. They all spent their days in a small space without any possibility of going out, not even to get some air. They had to wash in a tub that they each carried to the place where they believed they would have the most privacy. Children's clothing that became too small could not be replaced and if someone fell ill, they couldn't call a doctor. Meals were hardly varied and it was sometimes necessary to eat rotten food (Monday 3rd April 1944, Wednesday 3rd May 1944);
- Tensions within the group. Constantly living with the same people meant various kinds of conflict. Disputes were very common in the Annex ("To tell you the truth, I sometimes forget who we're at odds with and who we're not", Sunday 17th October 1943);
- Psychological pressure. The fear of being reported and arrested was in their minds day after day. As well as the countless precautions they needed to take every day (making no noise during office hours, never walking past a window, etc.), each bombing and burglary added to their stress. It was also very depressing and scary not knowing how long they would have to live under these conditions: "I can't tell you how oppressive it is never to be able to go outdoors, also I'm scared to death that we shall be discovered and shot. That is not exactly a pleasant prospect." (Monday 28th September 1942).

ANNE'S BEST FRIEND, KITTY

In her diary, Anne speaks to an imaginary friend, Kitty. Soon, Anne explains that she is writing because she doesn't have a real friend, even though she plays with her school friends. What she seeks is the opportunity to express her thoughts without restraint.

Initially, Anne mainly tells stories about her days spent at school or with people her own age. Once she is in hiding, however, the lack of people to confide in becomes a real weight for the girl to bear. Therefore, more than just a simple way to pass the time, the diary becomes an indispensable source of support for her, making life more bearable ("The nicest part is being able to write down all my thoughts and feelings; otherwise, I'd absolutely suffocate.", Thursday 16th March 1944). Writing also helps her to question her own personality. She claims to be able to analyze her own behavior as if it were that of another person (Thursday 6th January, Wednesday 12th January and Saturday 15th July 1944).

The Diary of Anne Frank therefore allows access to the thoughts written without any censorship, since they were intended for a friend who had to keep them a secret. It is undoubtedly because of this sincerity that the diary touched so many readers.

PUBLICATION AND RECEPTION

On the day of their arrest, Miep collected Anne's notebooks and scattered leaves of paper and locked them in a drawer with the intention of returning them to the girl later.

After the Liberation, Otto returned to the Netherlands. He learned of his wife's death but knew nothing of his daughters' and made efforts to find them. Finally, in July 1945, two sisters who witnessed the deaths of the Frank girls informed him of their fate.

Miep, then certain that Anne would not be returning, presented Otto with the writings. He did not read them until September 1945. Once he found the strength to do so, he was amazed to discover a daughter who was quite different to the one he knew.

After some hesitation, Otto decided to carry out his daughter's wishes: he planned to publish her diary. Initially, no publisher was interested. It was only after an article published by a historian in *Het Parool* newspaper that Anne's writings were released in a volume entitled *The Annex* in June 1947.

The diary was well received and 1500 copies of the first edition were quickly sold. The second edition was released in December 1947 and the third in February 1948. In 1950, the book was translated into German, French and English. In the United States, two adaptations, one theatrical and the other in film, were created.

FURTHER REFLECTION

SOME QUESTIONS TO THINK ABOUT...

- From the novel, try to identify the characteristics of an autobiographical narrative.
- What advantages does a subjective perspective present for a historical book?
- What kind of information can you find in the diary? Try to explain what drives Anne to continue writing this diary during her life in the Annex.
- The personal diary is a form that can be used to write fiction. Compare *The Diary of Anne Frank* with *Horla* by Maupassant. What are the differences between the two works? What does this form of writing contribute to each story?
- In your opinion, why is *The Diary of Anne Frank* one of the highest selling books in the world?
- The Frank family decided to break the law and go into hiding. However, nowadays, no one would label them criminals. What justifies their disobedience?
- What are the similarities and differences between *The Diary of Anne Frank* and the film *Mr. Batignol* by Gérard Jugnot?
- Anne Frank wrote her diary over 60 years ago, in a very different context from ours. Yet, some aspects of her life are similar to those of teenagers today. What are they?
- Write three pages of a diary of an Afghan child in Kabul, of a Palestinian from Gaza or of a young Tibetan monk.

FURTHER READING

REFERENCE EDITION

- Frank, A. 2001. *The Diary of a Young Girl: The Definitive Edition*. Reprint edition. Bantam.

REFERENCE STUDIES

- Anne Frank. *Une vie*, Fondation Anne Frank, Paris, Casterman, 1992.
- Lee C. A., *Anne Frank. Les secrets d'une vie*, Paris, Éditions de la Seine, 1999.
- Website of the Anne Frank museum created in the Annex : http://www.annefrank.org/
- Anne Frank Resource Center: http://annefrank.cidem.org/home.php

ADAPTATIONS

- *The Diary of Anne Frank*, animation by Nagaoka Akiyoshi and Julian Y. Wolff, 1999.
- *The Diary of Anne Frank*, telefilm by Jon Jones, 2008.

www.brightsummaries.com
ISBN ebook : 978-2-8062-7013-9
ISBN papier : 978-2-8062-7079-5
Dépôt legal : D/2015/12603/456

Cover: © Lisiane Detaille